# A Lunch With Punch

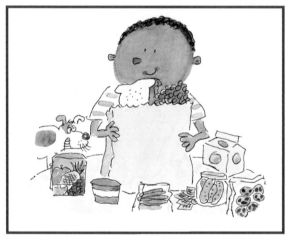

Written by Jo S. Kittinger

Illustrated by Jack Medoff

Children's Press®
A Division of Scholastic Inc.
New York • Toronto • London • Auckland • Sydney
Mexico City • New Delhi • Hong Kong
Danbury, Connecticut

For Joan Broerman with thanks
for her friendship and encouragement
—J.S.K.

To Lynn and Zack
—J.M.

Reading Consultants

**Linda Cornwell**
Literacy Specialist

**Katharine A. Kane**
Education Consultant
(Retired, San Diego County Office of Education
and San Diego State University)

Library of Congress Cataloging-in-Publication Data
Kittinger, Jo S.
  A lunch with punch / written by Jo S. Kittinger ; illustrated by Jack
Medoff.– 1st American ed.
    p. cm. – (Rookie reader)
Summary: A boy packs his lunch with delicious items, and then shares it
with a friend who has forgotten his own lunch at school.
  ISBN 0-516-22879-X (lib. bdg.)          0-516-27785-5 (pbk.)
  [1. Sharing–Fiction. 2. Food–Fiction. 3. Stories in rhyme.]  I.
Medoff, Jack, ill. II. Title. III. Series.
  PZ8.3.K65637Lu 2003
  [E]–dc21

                                    2003003762

© 2003 by Jo S. Kittinger
Illustrations © 2003 by Jack Medoff
All rights reserved. Published simultaneously in Canada.
Printed in the United States of America.

I pack my lunch.

Peanut butter
on bread.

# Add some jelly, thick and red.

# Money for milk.

Dimes and a nickel.

# A bunch of grapes.

13

14

# A sour pickle.

# A pudding cup.

# Carrots to crunch.

19

# Crackers for a snack.

# Cookies to munch.

# Juice or punch?

# Punch is fine.

# Zack forgot his lunch.

29

# Come share mine!

31

# Word List (46 words)

| | | | |
|---|---|---|---|
| a | fine | munch | snack |
| add | for | my | some |
| and | forgot | nickel | sour |
| bread | grapes | of | thick |
| bunch | his | on | to |
| butter | I | or | with |
| carrots | is | pack | Zack |
| come | jelly | peanut | |
| cookies | juice | pickle | |
| crackers | lunch | pudding | |
| crunch | milk | punch | |
| cup | mine | red | |
| dimes | money | share | |

## About the Author

Jo S. Kittinger, a native of Florida, lived in several states before settling in Alabama. A love of books and a passion to create inspires Jo to write both fiction and nonfiction books for children. Jo enjoys pottery, photography, and reading in her spare time. While teaching her own children to read, Jo realized the critical role of emergent readers.

## About the Illustrator

Jack Medoff's cartoons have appeared in magazines, news papers, advertisements, and commercials. He has also illustrated books for children and website cartoons. His work is on exhibit in galleries in Westport, Connecticut, and Rockport, Massachusetts. Jack has also worked as an art director for advertising agencies in New York and Los Angeles. He lives in Weston, Connecticut, with his wife, Lynn, his son, Zack, and his iguana, Zeke.